This Book Belongs To:

The Muppet Babies live in a nursery
in a house on a street that is a lot like yours.
But they can travel anywhere anytime using a special power—
the power of the imagination.
*Can you imagine* what it would be like to go with them?
Join the Muppet Babies on this adventure and find out.

Weekly Reader Presents

# Baby Gonzo's Treasure Hunt

By Joanne Louise Michaels • Illustrated by Tom Cooke

Muppet Press
New York

This book is a presentation of
Weekly Reader Books.

Weekly Reader Books offers book clubs for children
from preschool through high school.

For further information write to:
Weekly Reader Books
4343 Equity Drive
Columbus, Ohio 43228

One rainy morning, the Muppet Babies were eating breakfast.

"Gee," Gonzo said glumly. "It's raining so hard that Nanny will never be able to take us to the amusement park today. There's nothing to do in the nursery, and I'm bored."

"I'm sure you can find something to do if you use your imagination," Kermit suggested. "For instance, just look what's on the back of this box of Golden Treasure cereal. It's a real pirate's map!"

"That isn't a real map," Gonzo mumbled, eating another spoonful of cereal. "It's only a game on a cereal box."

Kermit shook his head. "Take a closer look."

Gonzo picked up the box and peered at the map.

As he studied the map, Gonzo felt the floor moving beneath his feet. When he looked up, he was no longer in the nursery. He was on the deck of a huge pirate ship anchored off a tropical island. The ship was the *Jolly Gonzo*! Around him stood his pirate crew. They were all pointing at the map in Captain Gonzo's hands.

"This map means silver…gold…jewels…real treasure!" bellowed the first mate, Mr. Kreegle.

"Aye-aye!" agreed the other pirates.

Gonzo shook his head. "No it doesn't. It's just a cereal box map, and I'm bored."

But the pirates wouldn't listen.

"This is no time to be bored!" shouted Mr. Kreegle. "We've found a treasure map. It's a pirate's duty to hunt for buried treasure!"

"Well...if you say so." Gonzo shrugged his shoulders.

The pirates all climbed into their longboat and rowed to shore.

"It says here," said Mr. Kreegle, looking at the map, "that we first have to cross the Oozyfenoozy Swamp to get to the treasure."

"Looks pretty tame to me," Gonzo yawned.

Before they all safely reached the other side of the swamp, Goldtooth Dan got stuck in quicksand, Pee Wee was nearly carried off by a giant pink flamingo, and a crocodile tried to take a bite out of Peg Leg's peg leg.

"I haven't had a crossing like that since the time a shark snatched Blackbeard's hat," roared Mr. Kreegle. "We chased that fish halfway across the Pacific Ocean to get it back."

Gonzo nodded his head. He couldn't say a word. He was still out of breath from his race with the crocodile.

"Now the treasure map says we've got to climb to the top of Mount Never Rest," Mr. Kreegle declared.

"Some mountains can be boring," said Gonzo.

But he had a strong hunch this one wouldn't be.

During the climb, three of the pirates almost fell off a cliff, Cutlass Kurt had a shouting match with a big brown bear, and Cross–Eyed Jack began an avalanche when he stubbed his toe on a boulder.

"I haven't made a climb like this since we escaped over the Andes Mountains chased by a band of wild mountain goats," Mr. Kreegle told Gonzo. "Those goats were fierce!"

"Wow," said Gonzo, dusting himself off. "That was some climb!"

Next, the map led them to the wide and dangerous Slamazon River. Captain Gonzo and the pirates built a sturdy raft and set off across the water. But the churning rapids caught them and whirled them downstream. The next thing they knew, they were going over a fifty-foot waterfall. Four of the pirates were swept overboard.

"At least they're all good swimmers," Mr. Kreegle observed as he helped the last of the pirates back onto the raft.

"Shiver me timbers!" Gonzo yelled. "This is really exciting!"

Finally, the pirates got to a sandy beach. "Here!"
Mr. Kreegle shouted. "We're supposed to dig for the
treasure at the X!"

All the pirates started to dig, with Captain Gonzo
working the hardest.

"Buried treasure," he thought as he dug. "This is
turning out to be one of the most amazing days ever!"

Clunk!

"I think I've hit something!" Captain Gonzo yelled. "Dig faster!"

Before you could say "Yo-ho-ho," the pirates had dug up an old treasure chest.

"I wonder what's inside," whispered Mr. Kreegle.
"Gold, doubloons, jewels...It could be the richest
treasure in the world. I haven't seen a decent treasure
since we dug up Blackbeard's mother's best silverware."

"Open it!" cried the pirates.

Captain Gonzo took a deep breath and lifted the top of the chest. All the pirates peered inside.

"Ah!" sighed Mr. Kreegle. "It *is* the richest treasure in the world—next to Blackbeard's mother's best silverware."

Gonzo stared into the chest. "What are you talking about?" he asked in amazement. "The only thing in here is Golden Treasure cereal!"

"That's right!" cheered Mr. Kreegle. "We're hungry! We just hiked through a swamp and were chased by a crocodile, and climbed a mountain and almost got eaten by a big brown bear. We rode a raft over a raging waterfall and dug up a pirate treasure, and we never stopped for breakfast."

Meanwhile, the other pirates were already taking out their spoons and bowls.

Gonzo watched as the pirates began to eat. He soon realized that he, too, was feeling very hungry. "After all," he thought, "I never finished *my* breakfast."

"Do you have an extra bowl?" he asked Mr. Kreegle.

Back in the nursery, Gonzo was finishing his cereal.
"Zowie, Kermit!" he said. "You were right. I just had
the greatest pirate adventure ever! I hiked through a
swamp and was chased by a crocodile, and climbed a
mountain and almost got eaten by a big brown bear.
Then I rode a raft over a raging waterfall and dug up a
pirate treasure."

"Not bad for a rainy morning," Kermit agreed. "And
you thought you were going to be bored."

"Bored?" Gonzo swallowed his last spoonful. "No way! Now that I've finished breakfast, I'm ready for another adventure. Would anyone like to join me?"